THIRTEEN
REMY CHARLIP & JERRY JOYNER

FOUR WINDS PRESS   MACMILLAN PUBLISHING COMPANY   NEW YORK

Macmillan Publishing Company
866 Third Avenue, New York, N.Y. 10022
Collier Macmillan Canada, Inc.
Printed in the United States of America
10 9 8 7 6 5 4
Library of Congress Cataloging in Publication Data
Charlip, Remy.
   Thirteen.
   Summary: Thirteen picture stories of a magic show,
a sea disaster, and other dramas develop separately
but simultaneously.
   1. Children's stories, American. I. Joyner,
Jerry.   II. Title.
PZ7.C3812Th   1985   [Fic]   85-3667
ISBN   0-02-718120-0

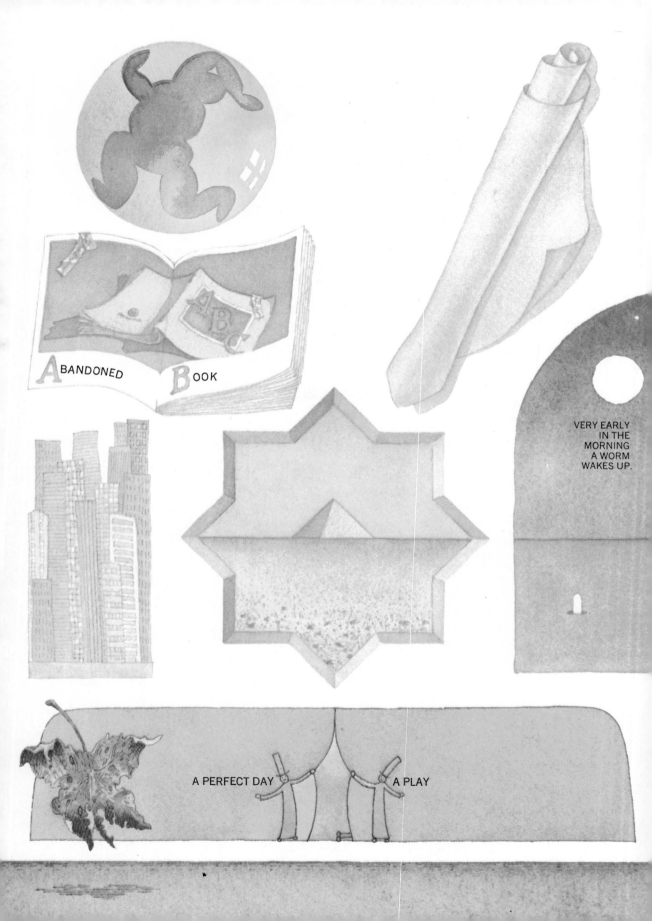

ABANDONED BOOK

VERY EARLY
IN THE
MORNING
A WORM
WAKES UP.

A PERFECT DAY   A PLAY

13

THIS IS A VERY OLD SHIP.

SWANS BECOMING WATER

VERY EARLY IN THE MORNING A WORM WAKES UP.

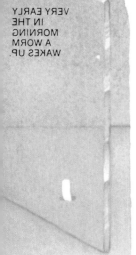

IT DOESN'T FIT

12

11

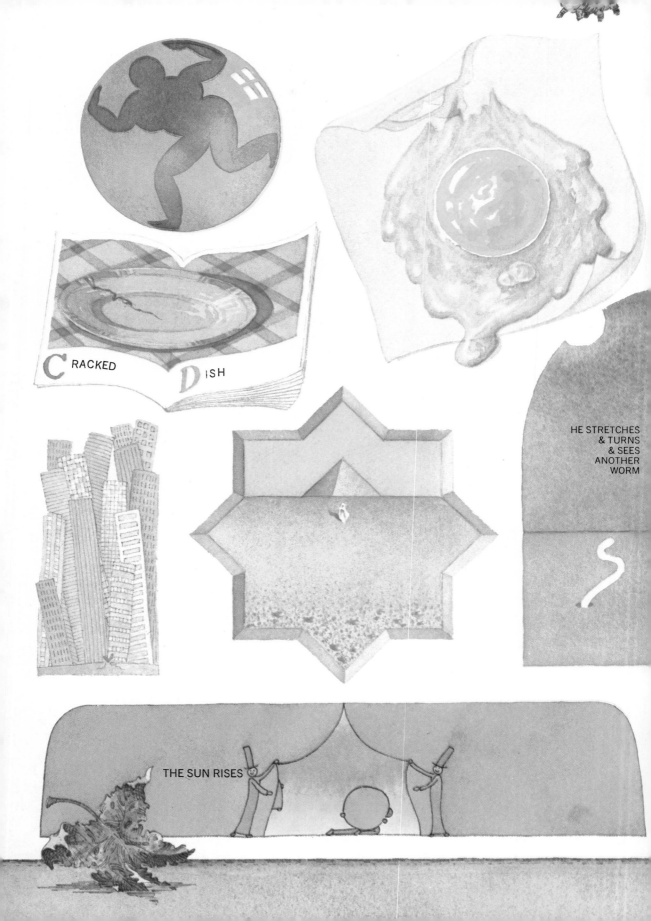

CRACKED DISH

HE STRETCHES
& TURNS
& SEES
ANOTHER
WORM

THE SUN RISES

12

WATER BECOMING STARS

HE STRETCHES & TURNS & SEES & ANOTHER WORM.

IN FACT IT'S SO OLD IT CAN HARDLY FLOAT ANYMORE.

IT DOESN'T FIT

11

E   F

10

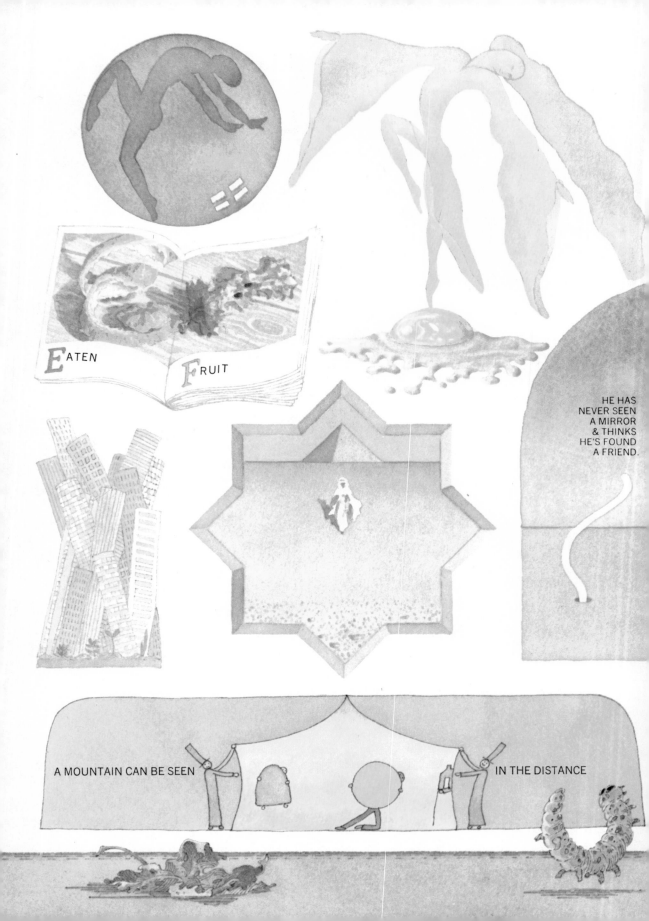

EATEN

FRUIT

HE HAS
NEVER SEEN
A MIRROR
& THINKS
HE'S FOUND
A FRIEND.

A MOUNTAIN CAN BE SEEN

IN THE DISTANCE

CHA... II

11

HE HAS
NEVER SEEN
A MIRROR
& THINKS
HE'S FOUND
A FRIEND.

STARS BECOMING TREE

IN FACT IT'S SINKING.

IT DOESN'T FIT

G   H

10

9

8

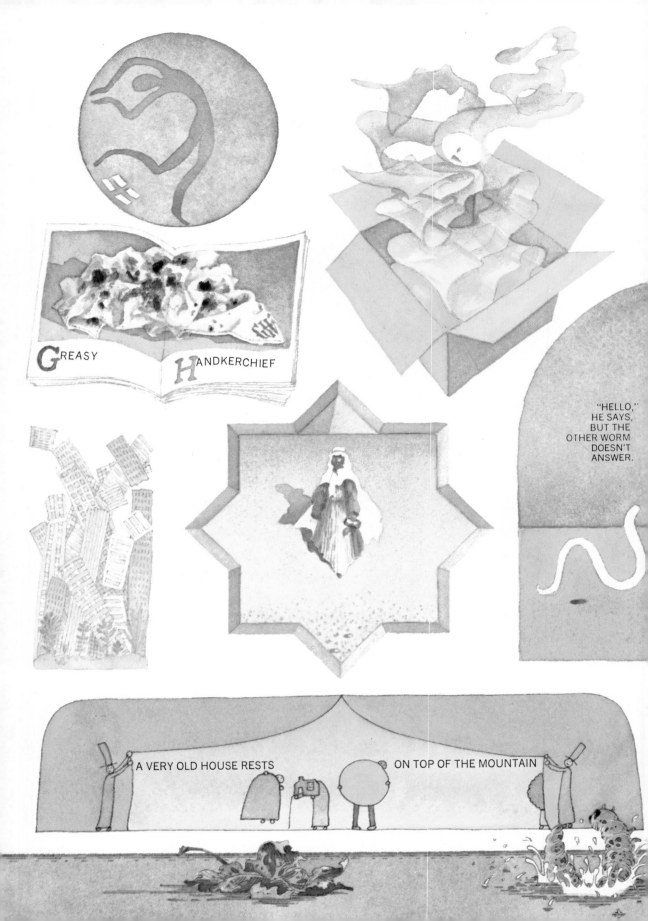

GREASY HANDKERCHIEF

"HELLO,"
HE SAYS,
BUT THE
OTHER WORM
DOESN'T
ANSWER.

A VERY OLD HOUSE RESTS ON TOP OF THE MOUNTAIN

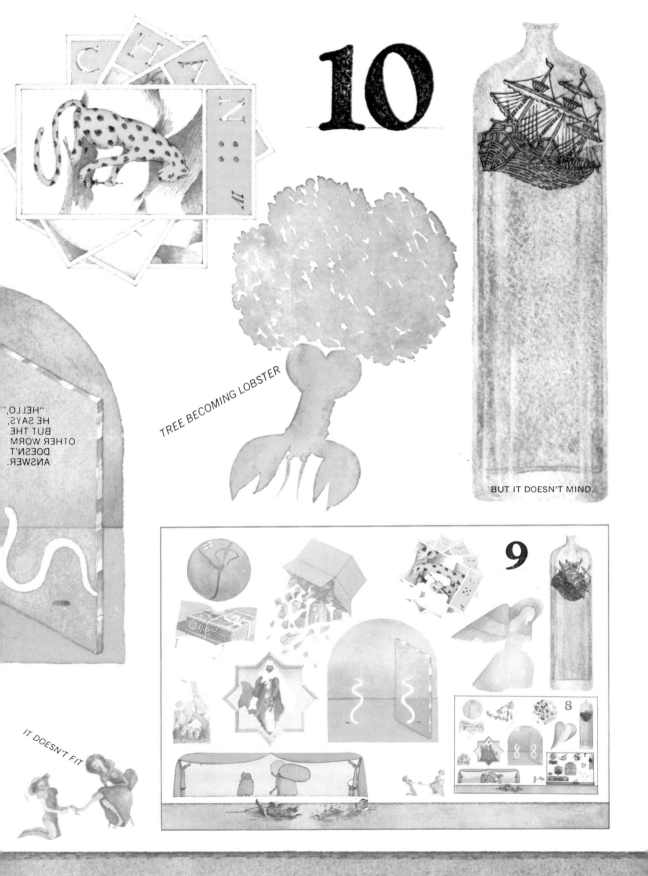

10

TREE BECOMING LOBSTER

BUT IT DOESN'T MIND.

"HELLO,"
HE SAYS,
BUT THE
OTHER WORM
DOESN'T
ANSWER.

IT DOESN'T FIT

9

8

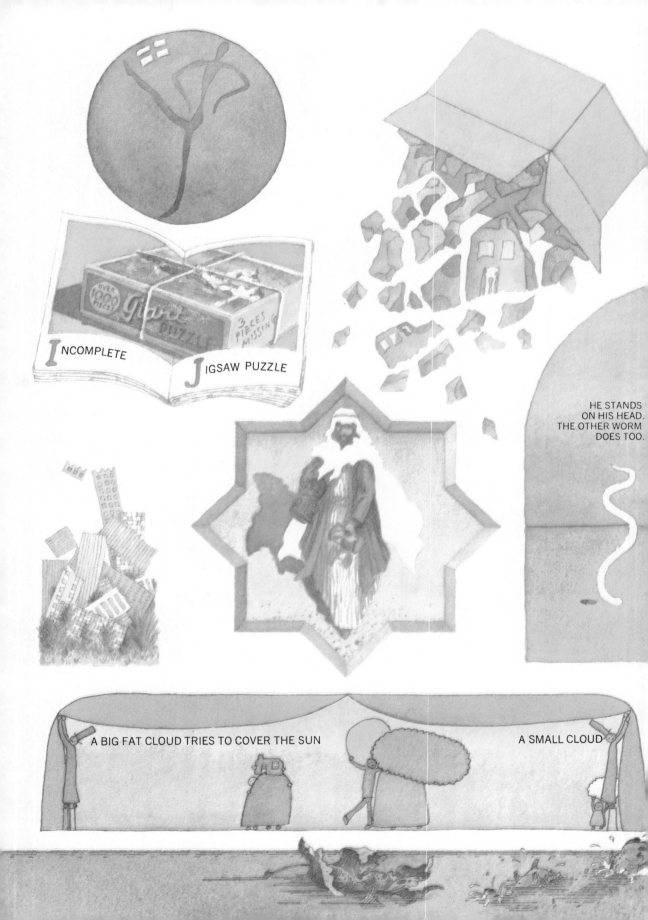

INCOMPLETE

JIGSAW PUZZLE

HE STANDS
ON HIS HEAD.
THE OTHER WORM
DOES TOO.

A BIG FAT CLOUD TRIES TO COVER THE SUN

A SMALL CLOUD

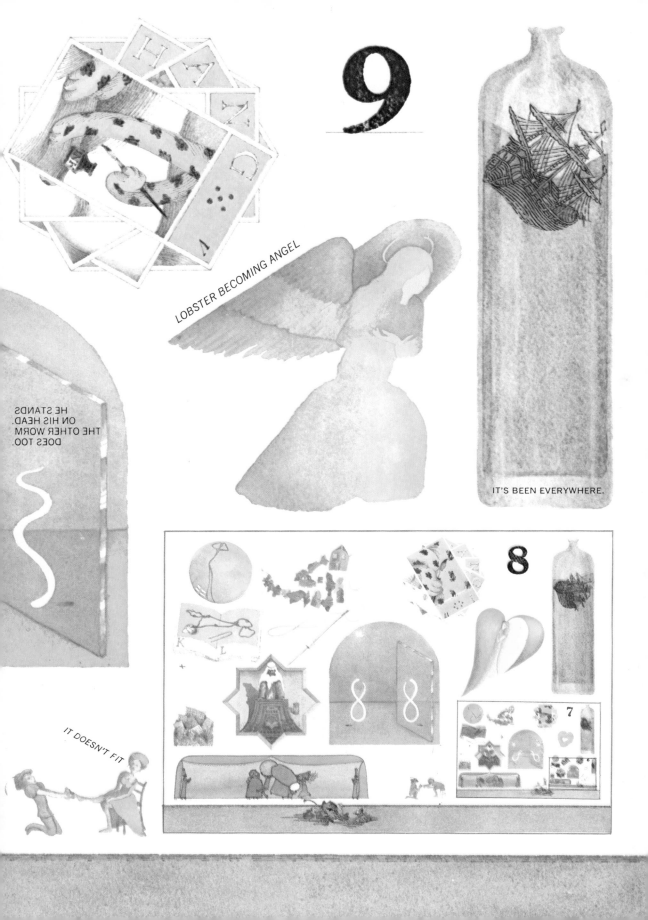

LOBSTER BECOMING ANGEL

HE STANDS
ON HIS HEAD.
THE OTHER WORM
DOES TOO.

IT'S BEEN EVERYWHERE.

IT DOESN'T FIT

9

8

7

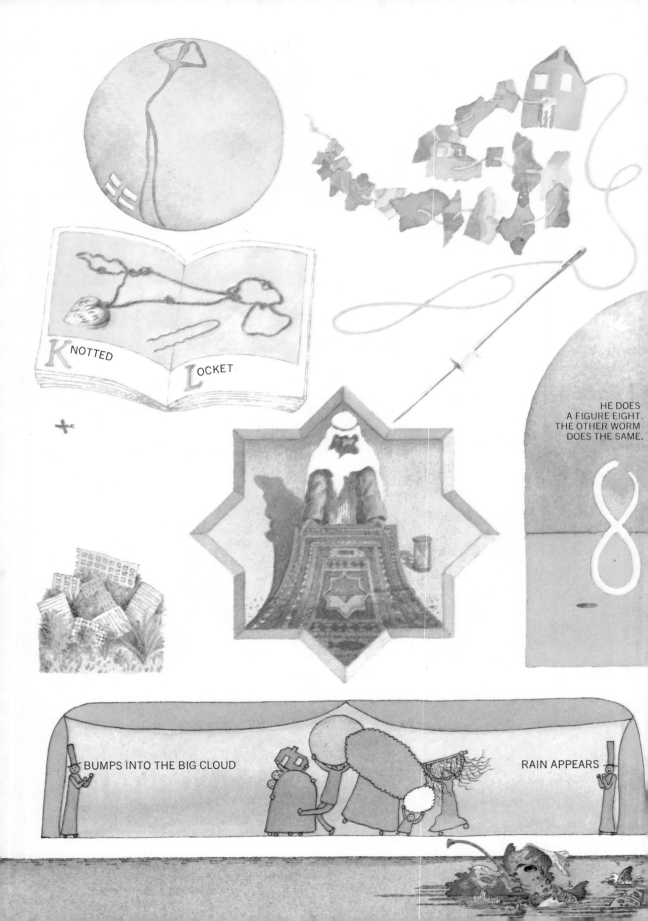

K NOTTED

L OCKET

HE DOES
A FIGURE EIGHT.
THE OTHER WORM
DOES THE SAME.

BUMPS INTO THE BIG CLOUD

RAIN APPEARS

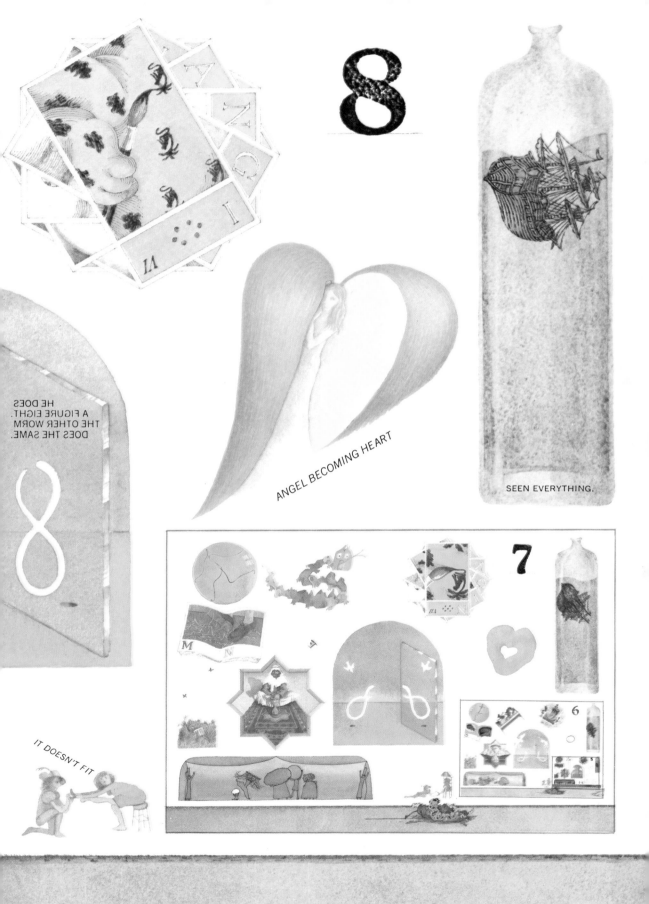

8

HE DOES
A FIGURE EIGHT.
THE OTHER WORM
DOES THE SAME.

ANGEL BECOMING HEART

SEEN EVERYTHING.

IT DOESN'T FIT

7

6

MASHED NOODLES

SUDDENLY HE SEES A BIRD DIVING FOR HIS FRIEND.

RAIN DANCES

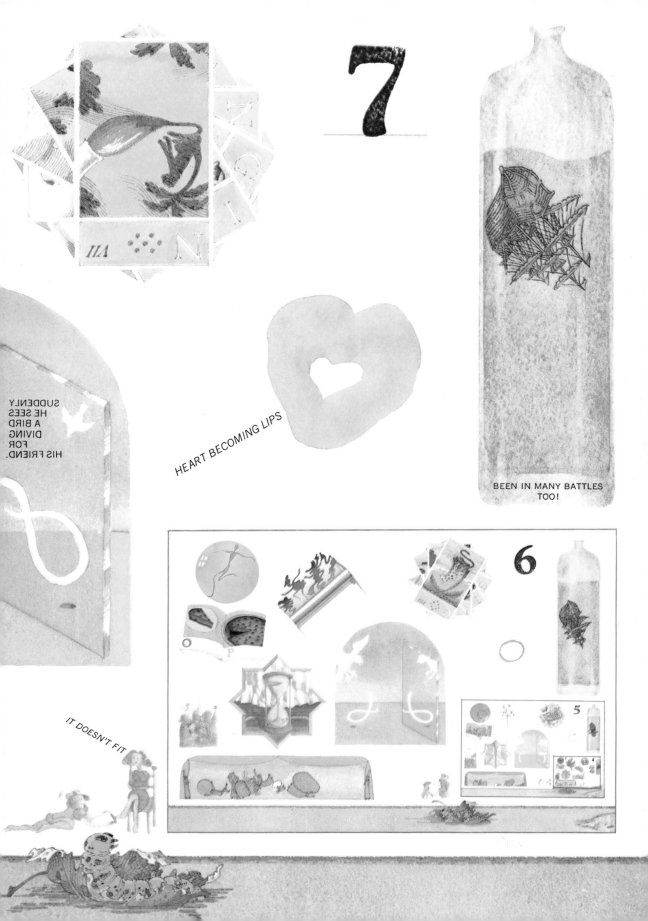

7

SUDDENLY HE SEES A BIRD DIVING FOR HIS FRIEND.

HEART BECOMING LIPS

BEEN IN MANY BATTLES TOO!

IT DOESN'T FIT

6

5

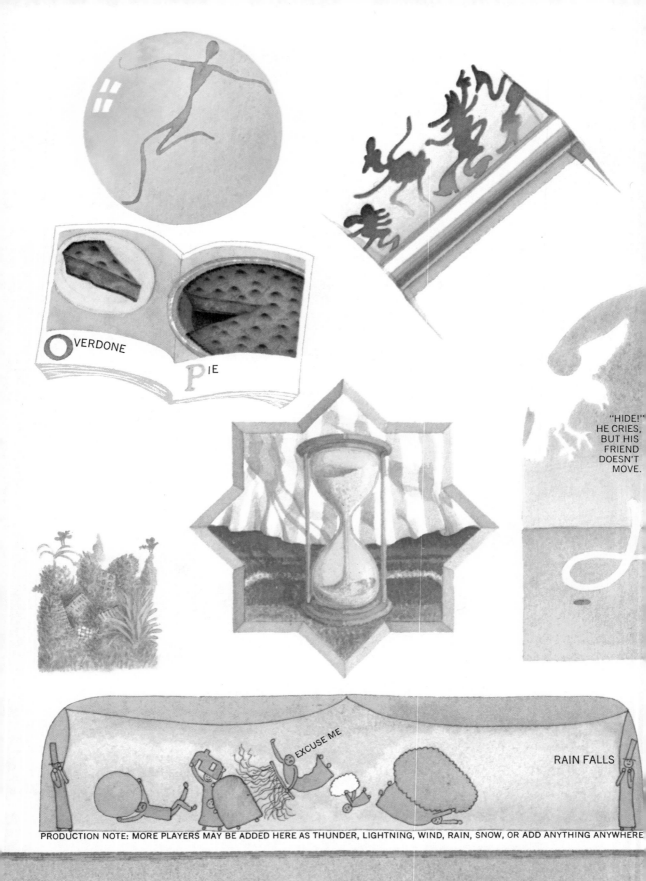

OVERDONE

PIE

"HIDE!"
HE CRIES,
BUT HIS
FRIEND
DOESN'T
MOVE.

EXCUSE ME

RAIN FALLS

PRODUCTION NOTE: MORE PLAYERS MAY BE ADDED HERE AS THUNDER, LIGHTNING, WIND, RAIN, SNOW, OR ADD ANYTHING ANYWHERE

6

TOO MANY.

LIPS BECOMING RING

"HIDE!"
HE CRIES,
BUT HIS
FRIEND
DOESN'T
MOVE.

IT DOESN'T FIT

5

4

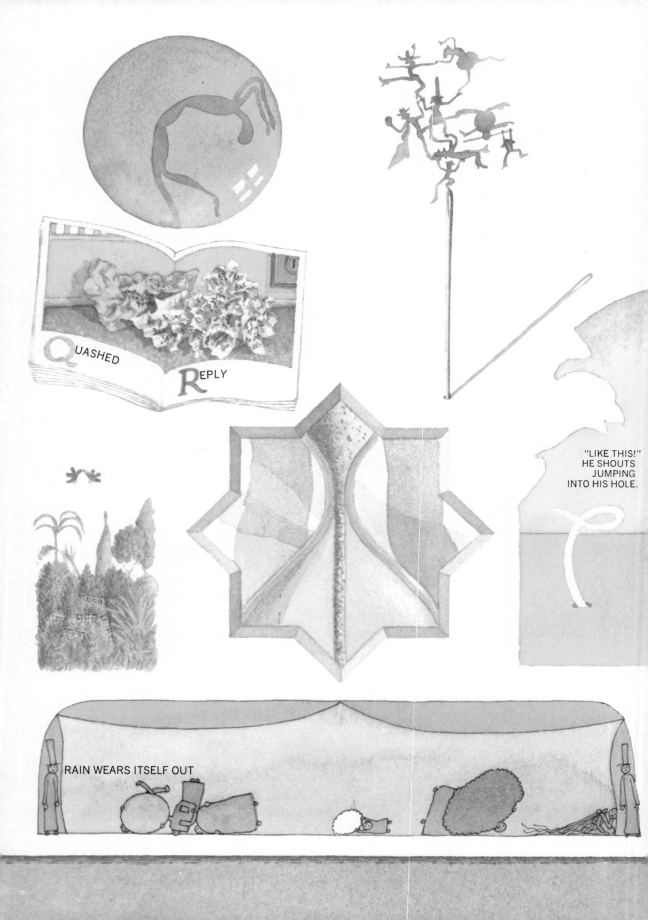

QUASHED

REPLY

"LIKE THIS!"
HE SHOUTS
JUMPING
INTO HIS HOLE.

RAIN WEARS ITSELF OUT

5

RING BECOMING LAMP

THAT'S WHY IT'S SINKING.

"LIKE THIS!"
HE SHOUTS
JUMPING
INTO HIS HOLE

IT DOESN'T FIT

4

3

SHATTERED TEAPOT

HE PEEKS OUT
& SEES THE BIRD
GOING FOR
HIS FRIEND.

RAINBOW

RAINBOW
RAINBOW
RAINBOW

RAINBOW

RAINBOW

RAINBOW

4

LAMP BECOMING ENVELOPE

AND ALTHOUGH IT HAS
BEEN AROUND THE WORLD,

IT DOESN'T FIT

3

2

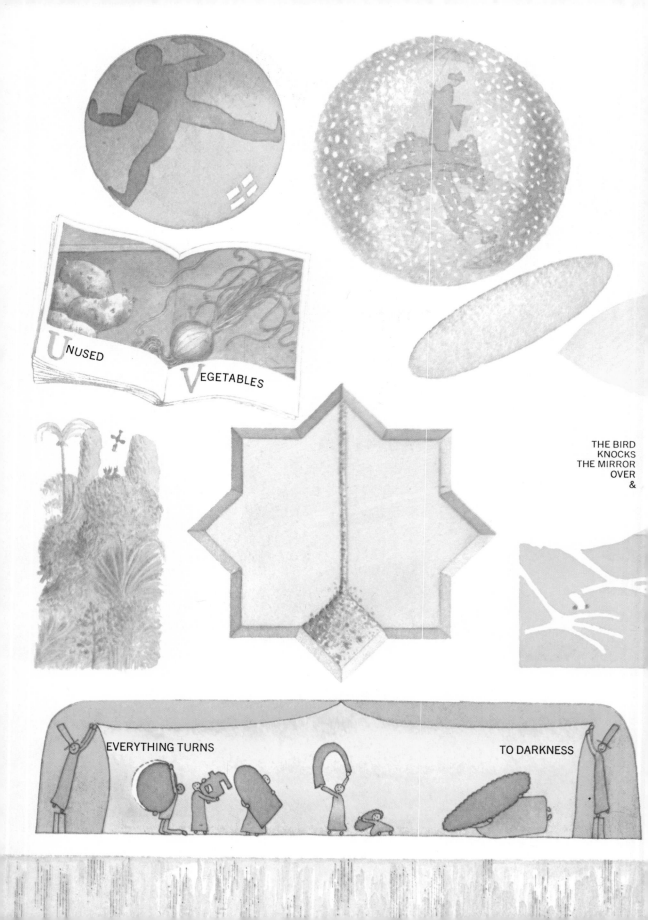

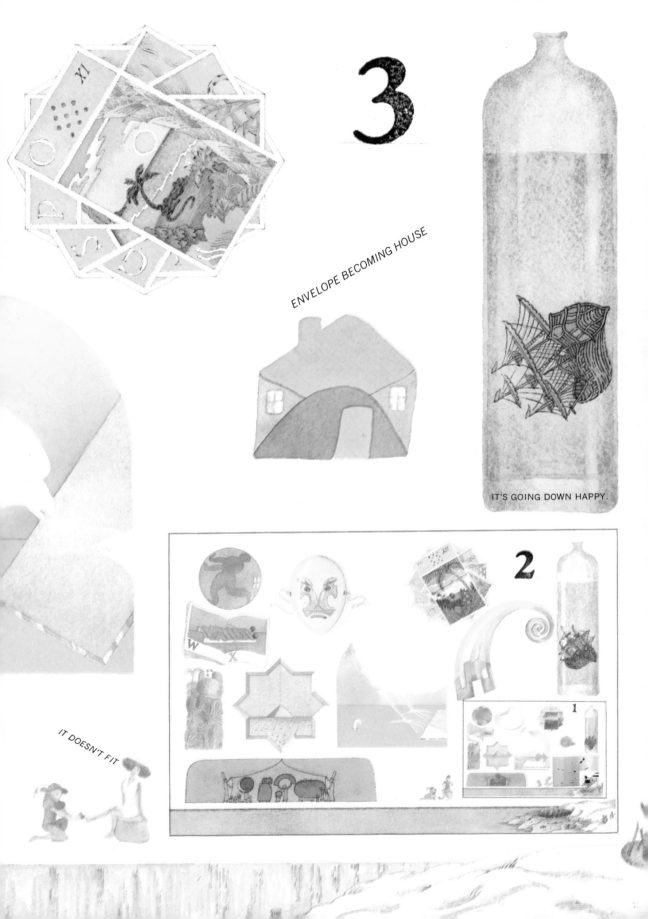

ENVELOPE BECOMING HOUSE

IT'S GOING DOWN HAPPY.

IT DOESN'T FIT

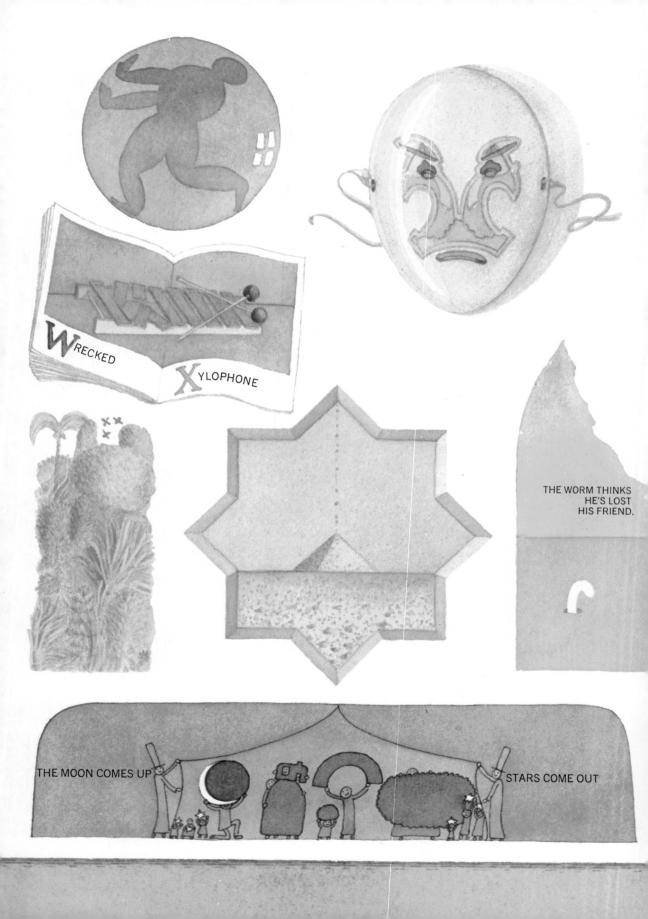

WRECKED **X**YLOPHONE

THE WORM THINKS
HE'S LOST
HIS FRIEND.

THE MOON COMES UP

STARS COME OUT

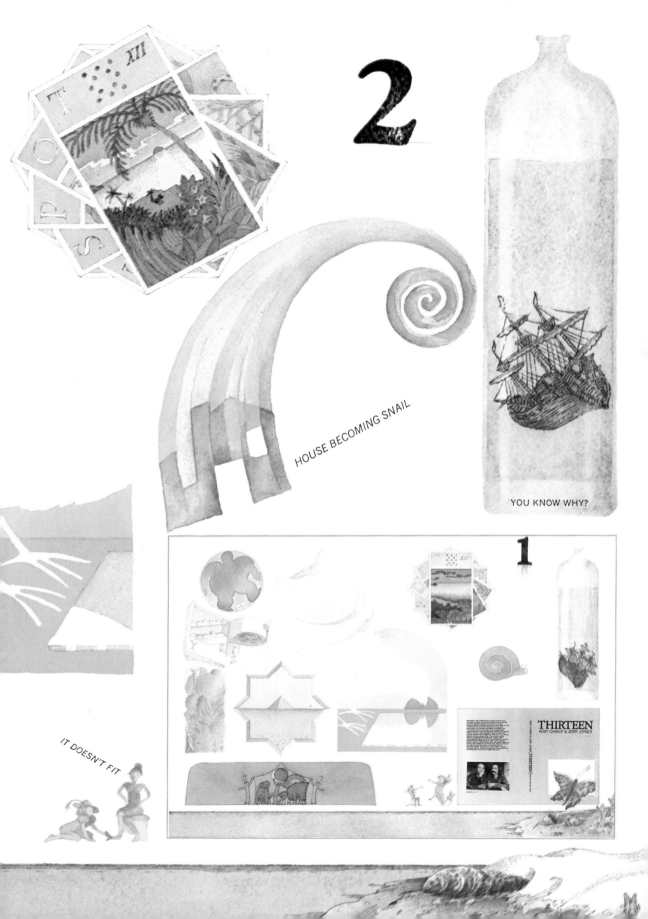

2

HOUSE BECOMING SNAIL

YOU KNOW WHY?

1

IT DOESN'T FIT

THIRTEEN
REMY CHARLIP & JERRY JOYNER

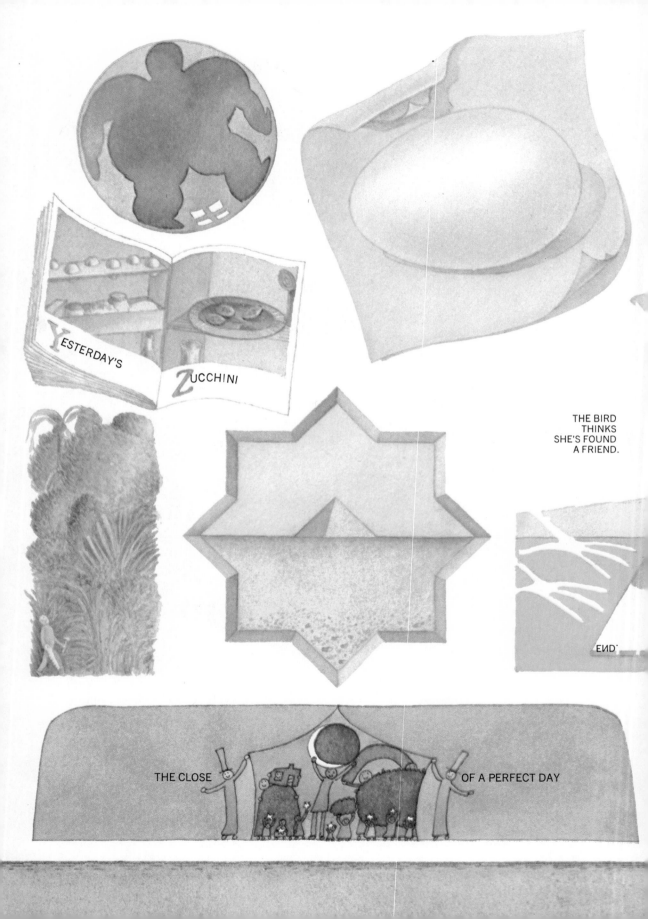

YESTERDAY'S ZUCCHINI

THE BIRD THINKS SHE'S FOUND A FRIEND.

THE END.

THE CLOSE OF A PERFECT DAY

1

S · XIII

SNAIL BECOMING SWANS

IT HAS NEVER BEEN TO THE
BOTTOM OF THE SEA BEFORE.

IT FITS!

REMY CHARLIP & JERRY JOYNER SHARED THE WRITING & PAINTING OF THIS
UNIQUE BOOK IN UNUSUAL WAYS & IN MANY DIFFERENT PLACES. IN NEW YORK,
MR. CHARLIP DESCRIBED HIS CONCEPT OF THIRTEEN TO MR. JOYNER &
SHOWED HIM SOME OF THE ORIGINAL STORIES HE HAD ALREADY BEGUN. OF THESE
THE SINKING SHIP AND THE GETTING THIN & GETTING FAT AGAIN DANCE
WERE INCLUDED IN THE FINAL BOOK. THEY DECIDED TO COLLABORATE, AND
IN THE YEARS & TRAVELS THAT FOLLOWED, THEY MET & CORRESPONDED
& WORKED SEPARATELY & TOGETHER DISCOVERING & DEVELOPING THE INDIVIDUAL
STORIES & THE OVERALL FORM OF THE BOOK. IN PARIS, NINE YEARS AFTER
THEIR FIRST MEETING, THEY SAT OPPOSITE EACH OTHER TO PUT IT ALL TOGETHER,
CHOOSING, SKETCHING, ADDING, CUTTING, FITTING, PAINTING & WRITING.
TWELVE OF THE SEQUENCES WERE DECIDED UPON. IN GREECE, DURING
THREE SUBSEQUENT MONTHS, THEY DID THE FINAL PAINTINGS. THE THIRTEENTH
SEQUENCE EVOLVED BY IMPROVISATION. MR. CHARLIP & MR. JOYNER EACH
PAINTED AN IMAGE ON A SEPARATE PIECE OF PAPER, THEN TRADING PAPERS, THEY
PAINTED A VISUAL RESPONSE TO EACH OTHER'S IMAGES. WORKING ALTERNATELY
THEY PASSED THE PAPER BACK & FORTH. THE FINAL RESULT WAS THE
PAPER MAGIC SEQUENCE. THIRTEEN IS REMY CHARLIP'S TWENTY-THIRD BOOK
(HARLEQUIN, HANDTALK, FORTUNATELY & ARM IN ARM) & JERRY JOYNER'S THIRD
(THE LOOKING BOOK & HOW FAR WILL A RUBBER BAND STRETCH?).

PHOTOGRAPH BY KEN FISK

THIRTEEN
REMY CHARLIP & JERRY JOYNER

REMY CHARLIP & JERRY JOYNER   THIRTEEN   PARENTS MAGAZINE PRESS